Cassie's Lost Hat

MARLENE R. ATKINSON

PAPERBACK: 978-1-7340699-6-9
EBOOK: 978-1-7340699-7-6

Ordering Information:

For orders and inquiries, please contact:
1-888-375-9818
www.toplinkpublishing.com
bookorder@toplinkpublishing.com

Printed in the United States of America

Cassie was very excited! She and her family were going to Grandpa and Grandma's home in the country to celebrate her birthday. It was a beautiful day and they were going to have a barbeque in the backyard. Before they ate, she got to open a big pink box. In it, she found a purple **hat** with a big yellow flower on it. It was beautiful!

Cassie tried it on and it fit perfectly!

Cassie wore her new **hat** to school. She told about it at "Show and Tell."

She wrote it shopping with her Mom. She wore it to piano lessons. She wore it almost everywhere she went.

She even wore it to bed!

The school year ended, and summer holidays began. Cassie's Dad and Mom loved car races, so they planned a trip to "Race City".

Mom packed a huge picnic basket and away they went, with Cassie wearing her **hat** - of course! When they got there, Cassie found some friends to play with. After a while, Mom brought out the picnic basket and they had a tasty lunch.

Races were very exciting for the family, but after a while Cassie got very tired, so she climbed up on her Moms' lap and fell asleep. She woke up just in time for the long trip home. When they finally got there, Cassie crawled into her bed and slept soundly.

The next day Cassie got dressed for Sunday school. She looked around for her hat.

She searched in her room. She looked in the kitchen. She checked in the porch and the car. It was nowhere in sight!

She began to cry! She probably left it at Race City! It was far too long of a drive for Dad to go and get it for her. After all, it's just a hat!

It turned out to be a sad day for Cassie! Not only did she lose something precious that Grandpa and Grandma had given to her, she would miss wearing the little hat that she loved so much!

Meanwhile, back at Race City, there was litter all over the place! There were pop cans, chip bags, candy wrappers, water bottles and all kinds of garbage left behind.

It was a big job for "Alma" the cleaning lady, to pick it all up.

Suddenly she noticed something purple! She picked it up and brushed it off for a closer look.

Wow! "What a pretty little hat," Alma thought! She wouldn't dream of throwing that away... so she brought it home.

9

The next day, Alma washed the **hat**. It came out of the wash machine looking almost like new!

She could only imagine how sad the little girl was that lost it; but on the other hand, it would make someone – somewhere VERY happy!

One day, Alma's friend came for a visit.

"Do you know anyone who would like this little **hat**," she asked?

"Margot," her friend, thought it was quite charming, so she decide to take it home for her daughter.

When Margot got home, she washed the **hat**, so it would be fresh and clean for her girl.

"Surprise," she shouted as Heather came through the door!

"Oh Mom, it's beautiful," cried Heather! "Where did you get such a pretty **hat**?"

"From my good friend Alma," Margot replied.

The next day, Heather wore her new **hat** to the gym. After exercising, she wore it to the pool.

Another day she wore it to her friend's house, then to the library and later to the grocery store. She felt good in that **hat**. She wore it everywhere she went!

13

Almost a year had passed, and Heather still loved that **hat**. One Saturday morning, she and her Mother took a bus ride to the center of the city to shop. They always had a great time shopping and usually topped off their day with ice-cream.

Time was getting on though, so they caught the bus to be home in time for Dad's dinner. By now, Heather was feeling sleepy and thirsty.

After a long bus ride, they finally made it home. Together they tended to the meal. Margot cooked, while Heather set the table.

Heather was daydreaming about their fun shopping spree, when suddenly she thought about her hat.

"Oh no," cried Heather, "I'm missing my hat!" Oh no indeed!

Meanwhile, back at the Bus Stop, a young girl and her two brothers were coming home from the Zoo. The boys waited on the bench, texting and listening to music, but their little sister was restless.

Marsha saw some pretty flowers near the trees and thought it would be nice to pick a bouquet for her Mom.

Off she went to get the flowers. Suddenly she noticed a **hat**! She picked it up and brushed off the dust and a few ladybugs.

"It was a wonderful **hat**," she thought!

When they got home, Marsha burst through the door shouting," Mom, Mom, look what I found at the Bus Stop!"

17

"Oh my goodness Marsha, it's a perfect fit," remarked her Mom.

Some young girl is probably pretty upset that she lost it," she said sadly, and you do realize we'll have to wash it."

So her Mom did some laundry while Marsha had a bath.

Marsha wore that **hat** everywhere-just like Cassie and Heather did. It was still very attractive and looked so cute on her!

She wore it to the corner store. She wore it to the library. She even wore it to the dentist and later walking through the Mall with her friends. They all thought the **hat** looked great on her!

Marsha and her friends from the neighbourhood were at the park one warm summer day. Suddenly the wind began to blow. It got stronger and stronger! Big black clouds formed and it began to pour! Leaves and branches were flying everywhere!

Suddenly someone shouted, "TORNADO!"

Everyone ran as fast as they could! Marsha scooped up her puppy and ran home as well! It was frightening!

By the time she got home, the power was out and her Mom was lighting candles.

"Oh, I'm so glad you're home, "cried her Mother!

"It's really storming out there! Tonight, we're going to have a picnic because I can't cook without power," she said.

Marsha's Mom served sandwiches, pickles and juice.

"It was fun to be eating by candle light," thought Marsha. She felt safe and cozy while the wind whistled outside. The storm raged on ferociously!

The next day, the sun shone brightly. Everyone had a good breakfast and talked about the storm and how scary it was. The wind had blown branches and leaves all over the yard. Thankfully, it hadn't been worse!

Marsha began thinking about all the things she could do today. Summer vacation was always so much fun! First, she would walk around the yard to check out all the fallen branches and leaves. She looked for her hat. It wasn't there!

"Oh no, she cried, I must've left it at the park!"

She ran down the street as fast as she could, with her puppy lagging behind! She looked and looked... NO HAT! She looked all around one more time. She found her soggy sweater, but still, NO HAT! It was gone!

Marsha walked home sadly with her puppy and went immediately to her room, flopped on her bed and cried. She loved that hat!

Meanwhile a few streets from the park, a little lady named "Muriel" was also glad the storm was over. She decided to walk her dog while she checked out the damage the storm caused in the neighbourhood.

Suddenly Sparky tugged at something in the storm drain.

"What is that Sparky," she asked?

He came running to her with something purple, wet and dirty. She realized then, that it was a "**hat**" as she turned it over in her hands.

When Muriel got home, she decided to wash the hat. She pulled of all the twigs and leaves and put it in the wash machine with a load of clothing. When she finished, the hat came out looking wonderful!

She always cleaned her clothes the old-fashioned way. Everything smelled so fresh, drying in the sunlight on her clothes line.

Of course, Sparky pretended to help her.

27

Days went by and Muriel could not think of anyone to give the little **hat** to, so she decided to donate it along with some other things to the Thrift Shop.

She got busy one afternoon and gathered enough of her own extra clothes, shoes and old purses to fill a huge box.

"Trouble is, how am going to get it there... it's sure going to be heavy," she thought!

Later that evening when supper was over, she relaxed, while sipping her tea and watching the news. She was quite exhausted after sorting all those clothes!

Sparky lay on the rug beside her. She really loved her dog! Not only was he company for her, he protected her!

29

Suddenly, there was a knock at the door...
"Come in," called Muriel.

There stood a young Girl Guide.

"Would you like to buy some cookies," she asked?

"Well, I was just wishing for a cookie with my tea," Muriel cheerfully replied.

The girl beamed, as Muriel went to get her purse.

While the Girl Guide waited, she noticed the huge box of clothes by the door. She couldn't take her eyes off it! She saw something purple on top of the pile. It looked like her **hat** that she lost long ago!

When Muriel returned with the money, she noticed the girl staring at the box.

Oh, those clothes are going to the Thrift Shop," Muriel mentioned.

Finally, the girl spoke up. "That looks like the purple **hat** that I lost a few years ago," she said.

Well, you're welcome to have it," said Muriel kindly. "In fact, could I ask you to help me carry the box to my car?"

The young girl – "Cassie," was so thrilled, that she ran out to get her Mother's help. Together, Cassie and her Mom loaded the box into their car. They agree to take it right to the Thrift Shop for Muriel.

On their way, Cassie tried on her long, lost **hat**. "Oh no Mom... it's too small for me now," she cried!

"Well, it has been a long time," said her Mother.

"I loved it so much when I was little, but if it doesn't fit me anymore then maybe someone else might like it," she said sadly.

"I'm proud of you Cassie. Let's just drop the whole box off at the Thrift Shop and you'll be making some little girl very happy somewhere," her Mother said softly.

"Goodbye my little **hat**," Cassie murmured, after hugging it one last time. She slowly walked away from the box of clothes and got back into the car.

CLOTHES

BOOKS

TOYS

SHOES & BOOTS

Puzzles

Trivia

33

Three months went by and the little hat was still in the big bin at the Thrift Shop with other hats, scarves, socks, mittens and a few toys. The little hat was a little lighter by now, but it was still attractive. So far, no one seemed interested in it. Maybe they didn't see it under all of the other things.

More time went by and one day a huge truck backed up to the big double doors at the back of the building. Some workers began to load the truck with all kind of things. They stuffed it with dishes, books, small furniture, toys, tools, clothes and of course, hats.

When the truck was loaded, it travelled through the city to the water front. There – they loaded everything into a large container and then the container was loaded with a huge crane onto a big ship.

The next morning, the ship set out across the ocean, bound for Africa. It took almost a week to get to the African shore.

People were very excited when it arrived. They gathered around to see everything that was being unloaded.

A lady and her little girl "Dianna" stood by and watched the commotion.

After a while, people left, carrying big bundles of thing they needed. They seemed very happy with what they found in the pile.

Suddenly, something caught Dianna's eye! She timidly walked over and picked out a little purple **hat** from the pile. She tried it on. It fit perfectly! She seemed VERY happy! It was the prettiest thing she had ever seen! It even matched her dress!

Dianna's Mother smiled warmly as she watched her fiddle with it this way and that. She loved that **hat**!

Dianna wore her new **hat** to market. She wore it to the river. She wore it to play with her friends in the village and later to the sea shore.

Dianna even wore it to bed! She wore that **hat** EVERYWHERE!

You see... this time the little **hat** made a long journey!

It made a lot of little girls very happy along the way.

It was still a wonderful little **hat** and fortunately, it was loved and treasured once again! It felt like brand new for Dianna!

CPSIA information can be obtained
at www.ICGtesting.com
Printed in the USA
BVHW022025241019
561996BV00016B/273/P

9 781734 069969